WANTED: PERFECT PARENTS

JOHN HIMMELMAN

Troll Medallion

Copyright © 1993 John Himmelman

Published by Troll Associates, Inc.

Published in hardcover by BridgeWater Books.

Designed by Leslie Bauman.

Printed in the United States of America.

10 9 8 7 6 5

Library of Congress Cataloging-in-Publication Data

Himmelman, John.
    Wanted: perfect parents / by John Himmelman.
      p. cm.
    Summary: A young boy describes to his real parents all the outrageous things his perfect parents would allow him to do.
     ISBN 0-8167-3028-8 (lib. bdg.)   ISBN 0-8167-3029-6 (pbk.)
     [1. Parent and child—Fiction.   2. Behavior—Fiction.]
    I. Title.
PZ7.H5686Wan   1993   [E]—dc20   93-22201

For my perfect parents—
Love,
Your perfect son

One evening, Gregory's parents saw a sign on their son's bedroom door. It read: WANTED, PERFECT PARENTS. INQUIRE WITHIN.

"I guess we had better see what this is about," said Gregory's father. They opened his door.

"Are you here for the job?" asked Gregory.

"Maybe," said his mother. "But what's wrong with the parents you have?"

"They make me do too many things I *don't* want to do and they don't let me do everything I *do* want to do," said Gregory.

"What would the job be like?" asked Gregory's father.

"Well, the first thing my perfect parents would do is *not* make me clean my room."

"But how would it ever get clean?" asked Gregory's mother.

"It wouldn't," said Gregory. "I would make tunnels and bridges out of all my stuff. It would be like a giant maze with secret caves hidden underneath. And only I would know the way in and out."

"But your parents would never see you again," said Gregory's father.

"Sure they would," said Gregory. "I would probably get hungry and thirsty. And when I did, my perfect parents would let me drink right out of the milk container and they would let me have every color ice cream in the world.

"I would make snowballs out of the ice cream and throw them up in the air and catch them in my mouth. The best part would be that my perfect parents would never say, 'Now save room for dinner, Gregory.'"

"Sounds messy," said Gregory's mother.

"Then I would take a bath, but I would take a bath *my* way. I would fill up the bathroom with water—all the way up to the window. Then I'd dive in and swim with big yellow ducks and hunt for sharks.

"My perfect parents would be right outside the door and they would say, 'We'd like to hear more splashing in there, please.' When I was done, I'd have my pet elephant drink up all the water."

"Your pet elephant? Where did he come from?" asked Gregory's father.

"My wonderful perfect parents bought one for me, of course. I would ride my elephant up and down the stairs and my perfect parents would say, 'What a lovely noise you are making.'

"Then I would put my elephant in for his nap."

"Where would your elephant sleep?" asked Gregory's mother.

"Under my bed, of course.

"But on clear nights, I would be sleeping on the roof anyway. And when the moon came out, I would howl like a wolf all night long because my perfect parents would never say, 'S*h*, Gregory, people are trying to sleep.'"

"Sleeping on the roof could be very dangerous," said Gregory's father.

"Not if my perfect parents surrounded the house with all our beds and couches and chairs," said Gregory. "If I rolled off, I would bounce right back up again and my parents would look out their window and say, 'Wow, that was a good one, Gregory.'

"And in the morning, all my friends would come over and we would have jumping contests. Whoever jumped the highest would get to eat a whole pizza, and whoever jumped the lowest would have to eat all the pizza crusts."

"I'd hate to be the loser," said Gregory's mother.

"Rules are rules," said Gregory.

"Then I would send everyone home, except for my best friend, Ernie. We would get out all my paints and we'd paint pictures on every wall in the house and my perfect parents would say, 'My talented son and his best friend, Ernie, are such good artists.'

"People would come from all around the world to see our paintings, just like in a museum. Someone might even buy all our walls for a billion dollars."

"Without the walls, what would hold up the ceiling?" asked Gregory's mother.

"It doesn't matter," said Gregory. "With the billion dollars, we would build a castle and surround it with a big moat.

"And my new room would be in a boat that sailed around and around the moat."

"What would you do with your elephant?" asked Gregory's father.

"It would be a real big boat, Dad. It would have to be to fit the 74 puppies and 43 cats that I would buy with the leftover money."

"Who would take care of your 74 puppies and 43 cats?" asked Gregory's mother.

"Let me guess," said his father. "Your perfect parents would, right, Gregory?"

"If they insisted," said Gregory.

"But I would bring all my pets to school with me. And I would give my teacher a note that said, 'My brilliant son, Gregory, is in charge of the classroom today. Signed, his mother and father.'

"Then the whole class would learn important things, like how to burp the alphabet and how to walk backwards without bumping into anything.

"Then we'd get on a big fire truck with a really loud siren and go on a field trip to the Amazon jungle and everyone would bring home a new pet.

"Then at the end of the year, we would bring all the animals back to the jungle. We'd live there until we got too many mosquito bites and had to come home."

"Sounds like fun," said Gregory's father.

"But here's the most important thing my perfect parents would do," said Gregory. "When I got tired, they would tuck me under my blankets, check for monsters under my bed, and say, 'Sweet dreams, my perfect child.'"

"Now *that* we can do," said Gregory's mother. "Sweet dreams, my perfect child."